Monica
and the Worst
Horse Ever

by Diana G. Gallagher

STONE ARCH BOOKS
a capstone imprint

Monica is published by Stone Arch Books
A Capstone Imprint
151 Good Counsel Drive, P.O. Box 669
Mankato, Minnesota 56002
www.capstonepub.com

Printed in the United States of America in Stevens
Point, Wisconsin.
032011
006106R

Library of Congress Cataloging-in-Publication
Data is available on the Library of Congress
website.

Library binding: 978-1-4342-1981-7

Summary: Monica and her friends from Rock Creek
Stables go on a trail ride, but will a lazy horse, an
annoying boy, and snobby kids ruin their fun?

Art Director/Graphic Designer: Kay Fraser
Production Specialist: Michelle Biedscheid

Photo credits:
Cover: Delaney Photography
Avatars: Delaney Photography: Claudia,
Shutterstock: Aija Avotina (guitar), Alex Staroseltsev
(baseball), Andrii Muzyka (bowling ball), Anton9
(reptile), bsites (hat), debra hughes (tree), Dietmar
Höpfl (lightning), Dr_Flash (Earth), Elaine Barker
(star), Ivelin Radkov (money), Michael D Brown
(smiley face), Mikhail (horse), originalpunkt
(paintbrushes), pixel-pets (dog), R. Gino Santa
Maria (football), Ruth Black (cupcake), Shvaygert
Ekaterina (horseshoe), SPYDER (crown), Tischenko
Irina (flower), VectorZilla (clown), Volkova Anna
(heart), Capstone Studio: Karon Dubke (horse
Monica, horse Chloe)

---------------------{ table of contents }---------------------

WELCOME BACK, MONICA MURRAY   SCREEN NAME: MonicaLuvsHorses

YOUR AVATAR PICTURE

— All updates from your friends —

 MONICA MURRAY is excited about going on the trail ride!!! Can't wait till Saturday! Hope Lancelot is ready for a long ride.

 CHLOE GRANGER: Lancelot is ready for anything. See you soon!

 CHLOE GRANGER can't wait for the trail ride! Rick-Rack can't wait either.
Monica Murray and 2 other people like this.

 OWEN HARGROVE III has a couple more days left of comfort before having to spend all weekend in the woods.

 MEGAN FITCH to OWEN HARGROVE III Do you think they'll let me bring my laptop on the trail ride?

 OWEN HARGROVE III to MEGAN FITCH I doubt it. Do you think they'll let us order sushi?

 ANGELA GREGORY has become a fan of Itsy Bitsy Betsey Beetle.

 TRACI GREGORY is tired. I'm cooking up a storm for Monica's trail ride this weekend.

 FRANK JONES: Yum. I hope you're making that potato salad your mom used to make.

 TRACI GREGORY: Yes, Dad, I am!

CHLOE GRANGER has become a fan of Rock Creek Stables.

 FRANK JONES Hi-yo Silver! Getting ready to go on a trail ride with my granddaughter and her friends.

> MONICA MURRAY: Can't wait, Grandpa!

 ANGELA GREGORY has scored 30,000 points in Itsy Bitsy Betsey Beetle Bingo.

 ALICE ORTEGA spent all week readying the stable and riders for the trail ride. Here we go. Hope nothing goes wrong at the last minute.

 RORY WEBER is looking forward to having time off this weekend. Everyone has to take care of their own horses, instead of me doing it. Yay!

Monica Murray and Chloe Granger like this.

 FRANK JONES has updated his information. He added "Senior Center Cowboys" to his activities.

 CLAUDIA CORTEZ to MONICA MURRAY Have fun this weekend! Tell me all about it on Monday.

Messages to MonicaLuvsHorses, Horses4Chloe, Guitar_Rory, OwenIII, Pretty_Megan, JenniferHeartsShopping

AliceAtTheStable said:
Meet at Rock Creek Stables on Friday. We need to have a meeting about the trail ride.

Chapter One

Silly Questions
and One Hurt Horse

Everyone at Rock Creek Stables was super excited. Along with another stable, Holly Hills Farm, we were having an overnight trail ride that weekend!

At the meeting, I sat between Chloe and Rory.

"Be here at seven o'clock tomorrow morning," Alice said.

Megan groaned. "Why so early?" she whined.

"We're leaving at eight, and you have to get your horses ready," Alice explained.

"That's Rory's job," Owen said, turning up his nose.

"Not this weekend," Alice said. "Everyone takes care of his or her own horse this weekend."

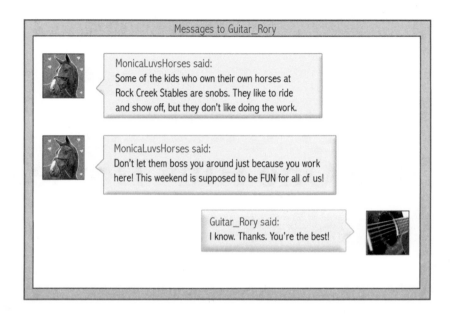

Messages to Guitar_Rory

MonicaLuvsHorses said:
Some of the kids who own their own horses at Rock Creek Stables are snobs. They like to ride and show off, but they don't like doing the work.

MonicaLuvsHorses said:
Don't let them boss you around just because you work here! This weekend is supposed to be FUN for all of us!

Guitar_Rory said:
I know. Thanks. You're the best!

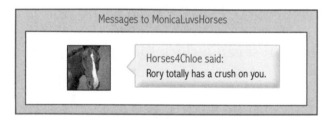

Messages to MonicaLuvsHorses

Horses4Chloe said:
Rory totally has a crush on you.

"We'll take trails and dirt roads to the campsite," Alice went on.

"We're staying on the Wilderness Preserve," Rory said.

"It's an empty field," Owen said.

"In the middle of nowhere," Megan added.

"That sounds creepy," Jennifer said. She shuddered.

I thought it sounded like fun. I'd camped out in backyards with parents and lights and a bathroom nearby. I'd never slept under the stars in the wilderness!

"The clearing won't be empty," Alice said. "Food, tents, and other gear will be trucked into the campsite."

"What kind of food?" Jennifer asked. "I can't eat beans or bologna." She gagged and made a sick-face. **"I'll throw up."**

"The Senior Center Cowboys are in charge of the Chuck Wagon," Alice said. "They'll have lots of good things to eat."

Jennifer didn't look like she believed her.

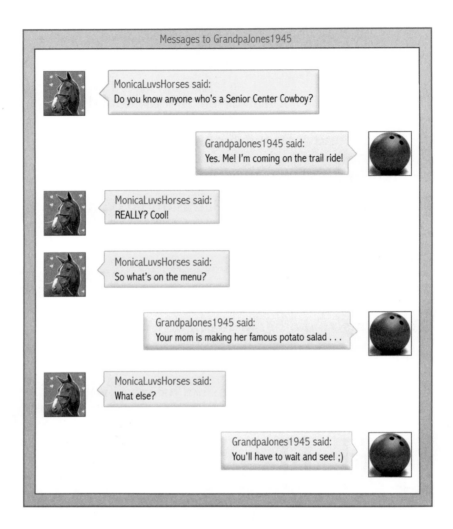

MonicaLuvsHorses said:
Do you know anyone who's a Senior Center Cowboy?

GrandpaJones1945 said:
Yes. Me! I'm coming on the trail ride!

MonicaLuvsHorses said:
REALLY? Cool!

MonicaLuvsHorses said:
So what's on the menu?

GrandpaJones1945 said:
Your mom is making her famous potato salad . . .

MonicaLuvsHorses said:
What else?

GrandpaJones1945 said:
You'll have to wait and see! ;)

"Are there bugs?" Jennifer asked.

It was a silly question, but Rory didn't laugh.
"We'll be outside," he answered. "So yes, there will be
bugs."

"I hate bug bites." Jennifer frowned. "They itch,
and I'm allergic."

"Bring bug spray," Chloe suggested.

"And if that doesn't work, we can use mud packs," I added. "You pack mud onto your skin, and it keeps the bugs away." I knew Jennifer wasn't going to like that suggestion.

"Gross!" Jennifer made another face.

"And don't forget," Alice said. "One horse will win the Most Valuable Horse trophy. If you want it to be your horse, take good care of him during the ride. We'll be there to help, but you need to do the work."

After the meeting, Chloe and I took Rick-Rack and Lancelot to a small pasture. We wanted our horses to work off some energy so they'd be calm on the trail ride. They ran and bucked as soon as we turned them loose.

"Why is Jennifer going on the ride?" I asked. "She hates outdoor stuff."

"Everyone else is going," Chloe said. "I guess she didn't want to feel left out."

"Do you know the kids from Holly Hills Farm?" I asked.

"I've met Savannah Summers and a few others at horse shows," Chloe said. "But I don't know them well."

I watched the horses play. Lancelot wheeled and then stopped suddenly. When he started walking again, he was limping.

My heart stopped. "Lancelot is hurt!" I whispered. Then I leaped over the fence.

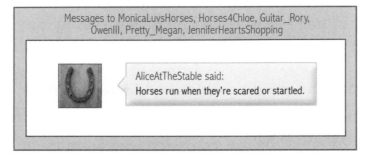

Messages to MonicaLuvsHorses, Horses4Chloe, Guitar_Rory, OwenIII, Pretty_Megan, JenniferHeartsShopping

AliceAtTheStable said:
Horses run when they're scared or startled.

I didn't run. If Lancelot jumped or bolted, he might make his injury worse. I held out my hand and spoke softly. "What's the matter, boy?" I asked.

Lancelot limped over to me. I held his halter while Chloe checked his leg.

"He's missing a shoe," Chloe said.

"Would that make him limp?" I asked.

"I don't know," Chloe said. "Let's ask Alice."

We took both horses back to the barn. Rory saw Lancelot limping and hurried over.

"What happened?" Rory asked.

I quickly explained. "I'll go get Alice," Rory said.

"I'll put Rick-Rack into his stall," Chloe said. "Be right back."

While they were gone, I scratched Lancelot behind the ears and tried not to worry.

Soon, Alice, Rory, and Chloe were back. Everyone was quiet while Alice checked Lancelot's hoof.

"He's got a bruise," Alice said. "He just needs a few days to rest, and he'll need some new shoes."

"Thank goodness!" I whispered.

"I'll call your mom and tell her what happened," Alice told Chloe. "We'll get the vet out here as soon as possible."

Chloe looked up sharply. "Wait a second," she said. "That means that Lancelot can't go on the trail ride!"

"No, he can't," Alice agreed.

"That's okay," I said, hugging Lancelot's neck. "I just want him to be all right."

"But we don't have an extra horse," Alice said. "I assigned the lesson horses to other riders last week," she added.

I was glad that Lancelot was going to be okay.

But I really, really didn't want to miss the trail ride.

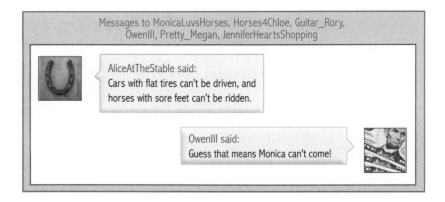

Messages to MonicaLuvsHorses, Horses4Chloe, Guitar_Rory, OwenIII, Pretty_Megan, JenniferHeartsShopping

AliceAtTheStable said:
Cars with flat tires can't be driven, and horses with sore feet can't be ridden.

OwenIII said:
Guess that means Monica can't come!

Chapter Two

Buck Barnaby's
Old Plug

When I got home, Mom was in the kitchen. She was peeling potatoes for the potato salad. Angela, my bratty eight-year-old stepsister, sat at the kitchen table. She was eating a sandwich.

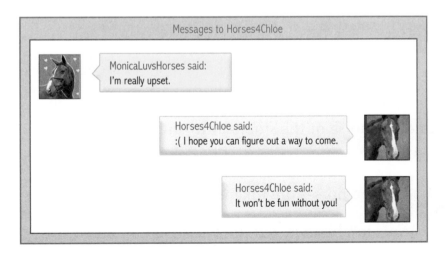

Messages to Horses4Chloe

MonicaLuvsHorses said:
I'm really upset.

Horses4Chloe said:
:(I hope you can figure out a way to come.

Horses4Chloe said:
It won't be fun without you!

"What's wrong?" Mom asked. She knew right away that I was upset.

Our dog, Buttons, knew something was wrong, too. Buttons shoved her nose in my hand and whined.

Angela could tell I was upset, but she wasn't worried about me. Just curious. "Did you fall off your horse?" she asked.

"Sort of. Lancelot lost a shoe and hurt his foot," I explained.

"Can't he get new shoes and put on a Band-Aid?" Angela asked.

Mom laughed. "It's different for horses, sweetie," she said. Then she turned to me. "Will Lancelot be okay?" she asked.

"Yes, but I can't ride him for a few days," I said.

Mom frowned. "What about the trail ride? Is there another horse at the stable that you can borrow?" she asked.

"All the horses are taken," I said. "I can't go."

Angela's head jerked up. She asked, "Will you be home all day tomorrow?"

"I guess so," I told her. I sighed and sat down.

"You can't watch TV!" Angela shrieked. "There's an *Itsy Bitsy Betsey Beetle* movie on tomorrow!"

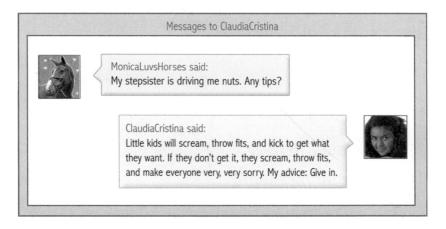

Messages to ClaudiaCristina

MonicaLuvsHorses said:
My stepsister is driving me nuts. Any tips?

ClaudiaCristina said:
Little kids will scream, throw fits, and kick to get what they want. If they don't get it, they scream, throw fits, and make everyone very, very sorry. My advice: Give in.

I hate *Itsy Bitsy Betsey Beetle* cartoons. The bugs have annoying teeny tiny voices, and they sing stupid songs. But Angela's screech is worse. And she breaks stuff when she's mad.

Besides, winning a Betsey Beetle battle wouldn't make me feel better about missing the trip.

"You can watch your show," I said. "I don't care."

Mom put the potatoes on the stove to boil. "Do you want a tuna sandwich, Monica?" she asked.

"Yes, thank you," I said. "With pickles, please." A tuna sandwich wouldn't make me feel better, either, but I was hungry.

I was still eating when Grandpa Jones got home.

"Is the potato salad done?" Grandpa asked.

"Nope. You can have some for dinner," Mom said. "How was your meeting?"

"The Senior Center Cowboys are all set to hit the trail tomorrow." Grandpa chuckled. "I think we're more excited than the kids."

Mom gave me a quick look. "Monica's not going to be able to go," she told Grandpa. "Lancelot got hurt today, and there's not another horse for her to ride."

Grandpa's face fell. "That takes the fun out of it for me!" he told me. "Maybe I'll stay home, and we can do something fun together. I didn't want to hang out with all those old people anyway." He winked at me.

That gave me an idea. I couldn't ride a horse on the trail ride, but maybe I didn't have to miss it.

"Do you think the Chuck Wagon might have room for one more volunteer?" I asked.

Grandpa frowned and rubbed his chin. He does that when he's thinking.

"I can help you cook," I said quickly. "And Alice might need help with the lesson horses."

"I don't think there's room in the trucks," Grandpa said. "But I might have something better. Let me make a phone call."

Grandpa left the room. "What do you think his idea is?" Mom asked.

I shrugged. "Maybe he'll ask if someone can make room for me in their truck," I said.

Angela wrinkled her nose. "Gross. I don't know why you want to go on the dumb trail ride anyway. You're going to get so dirty!"

Mom winked at me. "That's part of the fun," she told Angela.

Angela looked disgusted.

Before she could say anything else, Grandpa walked back in. He was grinning. "Good news!" he said. "My pal Buck Barnaby will let you ride his horse this weekend."

I squealed and threw my arms around his neck. "Thank you so much!" I said. "You're the best grandpa in the world."

Grandpa Jones smiled and pulled his car keys out of his pocket. "Let's go meet Joker," he said.

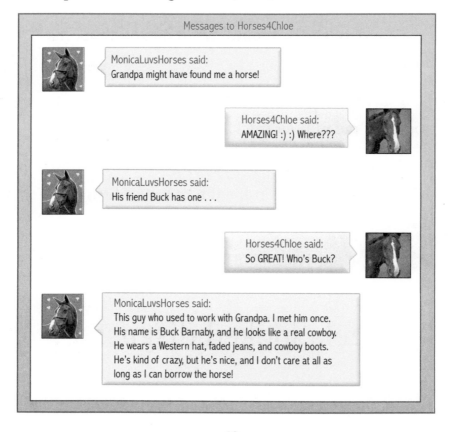

Messages to Horses4Chloe

MonicaLuvsHorses said:
Grandpa might have found me a horse!

Horses4Chloe said:
AMAZING! :) :) Where???

MonicaLuvsHorses said:
His friend Buck has one . . .

Horses4Chloe said:
So GREAT! Who's Buck?

MonicaLuvsHorses said:
This guy who used to work with Grandpa. I met him once. His name is Buck Barnaby, and he looks like a real cowboy. He wears a Western hat, faded jeans, and cowboy boots. He's kind of crazy, but he's nice, and I don't care at all as long as I can borrow the horse!

When Grandpa and I got to Buck Barnaby's farm, he was standing outside. He and Grandpa shook hands.

"I put the old plug in a stall," Buck said.

I blinked. An old plug? That didn't sound good.

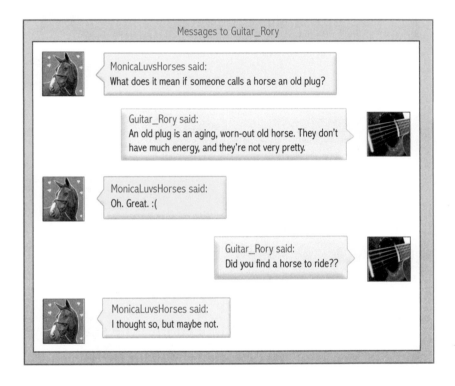

Messages to Guitar_Rory

MonicaLuvsHorses said:
What does it mean if someone calls a horse an old plug?

Guitar_Rory said:
An old plug is an aging, worn-out old horse. They don't have much energy, and they're not very pretty.

MonicaLuvsHorses said:
Oh. Great. :(

Guitar_Rory said:
Did you find a horse to ride??

MonicaLuvsHorses said:
I thought so, but maybe not.

"How old is Joker?" I asked.

"Ten," Buck told me. He laughed. "I just call him an old plug because I'm an old man. Makes me feel better."

I smiled and relaxed.

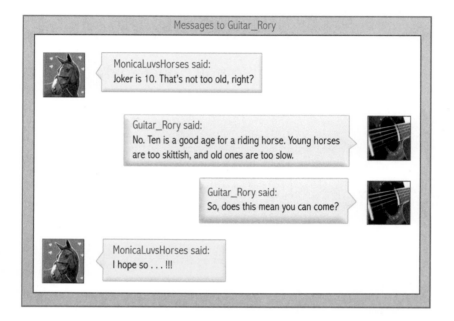

We walked into the barn. It was full of farm equipment. Joker's stall was at the far end.

"Wake up, Joker!" Buck called out.

My eyes popped when I looked into the stall. Joker's brown coat was splattered with mud. His short black mane was tangled. He had long whiskers on his nose and long hair on his legs.

"How are you, boy?" Grandpa asked. He held his hand out.

Joker didn't look up. He just swished his short, scraggly tail.

"You need a carrot to get his attention," Buck said. He pulled a carrot out of his pocket and handed it to me.

I held out the carrot. Joker didn't step forward to get the treat. He stretched out his neck. He didn't want to move, not even for a carrot.

Then I saw the clunky old saddle in the next stall.

"Is that Joker's tack?" I asked.

"Yep." Buck looked at his watch. "It's feeding time," he told us. "I'll be right back."

When Buck was gone, Grandpa smiled at me. "What do you think?" he asked. "Isn't this great? Now you can go on the trail ride!"

"I can't ride Joker on the trail ride!" I whispered. I didn't want Buck to hear.

Grandpa frowned. "Why can't you?" he asked.

"He's lazy and dirty and small," I said. "Riding him would be too embarrassing."

"I thought you didn't care what other people think," Grandpa said. "You always say the horse snobs at the barn are so awful."

I stared at him.

He was right.

I sounded just like the horse snobs!

"Joker doesn't look like much, but he's perfect for a cross-country ride," Grandpa said. "You've got two choices, Monica. You can stay home, or you can ride Joker."

I didn't think Joker was perfect, but I didn't want to be a horse snob. And I definitely didn't want to stay home.

"You're right," I said. "I'd rather ride Joker than stay home."

Messages to Guitar_Rory, Horses4Chloe

MonicaLuvsHorses said:
I'm coming on the trail ride!!!!!!!!!!!!!!!!!!!!

Chapter Three

Joker
Isn't a Joke

I drove to the barn with Grandpa on Saturday morning. A lot of kids were already there, loading their stuff into a pick-up truck. Each rider was allowed to bring one backpack and a sleeping bag.

"My bug spray, bite medicine, and mosquito net won't fit in my backpack," Jennifer said. "I'm allergic. I have to have them. Can't I bring two bags?"

Megan frowned at Jennifer. "They won't let me bring my games and snacks or an extra blanket," Megan said. "I'll be cold, hungry, and bored, but I'm not whining."

"I'll be a gigantic itchy spot!" Jennifer screeched. She sounded hysterical.

"Megan, games, snacks, and a blanket are not the same thing as needing medicine," Alice told Megan. "Jennifer, you can bring the stuff you need."

Megan stomped away.

Alice and Rory helped the lesson kids saddle up. The horse owners were getting ready in the barn. Six other kids were brushing horses by a horse van.

"Are those kids from Holly Hills?" I asked Chloe.

Chloe nodded and pointed to a tall man with blond hair. "That's Chase Hogan, the Holly Hills trainer," she told me. She pointed at a tall, pretty brown-haired girl. "And that's Savannah Summers," Chloe added, whispering. "I know her from going to shows. She's not exactly nice."

Buck hadn't arrived with Joker yet, so I helped Chloe with Rick-Rack. She brushed one side of the horse, and I brushed the other.

"Did you bring a bathing suit?" Chloe asked me as we brushed Rick-Rack.

Savannah heard her. "Is there a pool?" she asked.

"There's a pond," Chloe said. "We can take our horses swimming."

I hoped Joker liked water. This might be my only chance ever to swim with a horse. I couldn't wait.

Savannah made a face. "I'm not swimming in scummy pond water," she said. "And I'd never let Blue Magic get all icky!"

I gave Lancelot a carrot and patted his nose. "I wish you were coming with me, buddy," I told him. "Hope you get some rest."

Then I followed Chloe and Rick-Rack out of the barn. Most of the riders were outside when Buck drove in. So everyone watched Joker back out of the trailer.

Joker was still short and stocky with whiskers and shaggy legs, but at least today he was clean. Buck had combed out his mane and tail and polished the saddle.

Some of the horse snobs giggled and whispered as Buck led Joker out of the trailer.

"Who's riding the runt?" Owen asked.

Savannah giggled.

"Who'd want to?" Megan said, laughing.

"Me," I said.

"I am. And I want to."

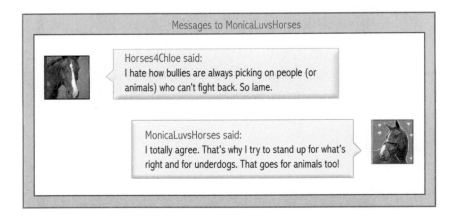

I walked over and took Joker's reins. "Thanks, Buck," I said. "I'll take good care of him."

Buck smiled at me. "I know you will, Monica," he said. "See you tomorrow."

I walked the horse over to Chloe and Rick-Rack.

"What's his name?" Chloe asked.

"Joker," I said.

"That's a good name. He is a joke," Megan said. "Look how slow he is!"

"He's a cow pony!" Savannah exclaimed.

"I think he's cute," Chloe said. "And his saddle looks comfortable."

Chloe was trying to make me feel better. That was nice, but facts were facts. Joker was scruffy-looking and lazy.

"I like your mangy mustang, Monica," Owen said. "Less competition for me. There's no way he'll win the Most Valuable Horse trophy."

Owen, Megan, and Savannah left to join the other snobby owners.

"Who needs a stupid award?" Chloe exclaimed. "You're coming on the trail ride, Monica. That's all I care about."

"He's a good horse," Rory told me. "You won't be sorry you rode him." I smiled, but I knew he was trying to make me feel better too.

MonicaLuvsHorses said:
Rory is a walking horse encyclopedia!

Horses4Chloe said:
I know. He's so smart.

Horses4Chloe said:
He's also GORGEOUS!!! ;)

MonicaLuvsHorses said:
Okay, I admit it, he is pretty cute . . .

Horses4Chloe said:
I KNEW IT!!!

Horses4Chloe said:
YOU LIKE HIM!!!!!

MonicaLuvsHorses said:
Quit it, Chloe. We're just friends!

Horses4Chloe said:
Okay, okay. But I think he likes you. And you'd be a really cute couple.

MonicaLuvsHorses said:
I'm ignoring you now!!!

Alice told everyone to mount up.

"Let's get going," she said. "We want to use all the daylight we can."

Joker didn't move when I put my foot in the stirrup. He stood still while I got on, and he stayed quiet while I waited.

Rick-Rack pranced as Chloe swung onto his back. "Easy, boy," she said softly.

He stopped jiggling.

When Megan put her foot in the stirrup, Dandy backed up. Megan hopped on one foot, shouting, "Whoa! Stop!" Alice gave her a boost onto Dandy's back.

Every time Owen tried to mount, Merlin started walking. Owen hopped, sprang, flopped across the saddle, and finally pulled himself on.

Savannah led Blue Magic to the mounting stool. His gray coat sparkled, and his black mane and tail were shiny clean. But he wouldn't stay near the mounting stool. Rory had to hold him so Savannah could get on.

I patted Joker's neck and smiled.

"Good boy,"

I whispered.

The ride hadn't even started, and I was already glad I was riding Buck's little horse. I was the only person who hadn't had a hard time so far.

Chapter Four

Ethan Westfield
from Holly Hills

Mark Bristow, the Rock Creek trainer, moved his arm like he was throwing a ball. That was the signal to start moving.

Mark and Chase rode at the front of the line. There were six Holly Hills Farm riders, six Rock Creek owners, and four Rock Creek lesson kids, counting me. Alice and Rory spaced themselves between us. Rory is fourteen, but he works at the barn, so he doesn't count as one of the kids.

At first, Chloe and I were riding in the middle of the group. But then we had to walk single file on the trail through the woods.

That's when the trouble started.

"Get that stupid pony moving!" Owen complained from behind us.

"You're holding up the line!" someone else shouted.

I glanced back, and Savannah was glaring at me. "At this speed, it'll be dark when we get to the campsite," she said.

The jokes were embarrassing, but they were also true. Joker walked too slowly. I kicked him into a jog, but it didn't help much.

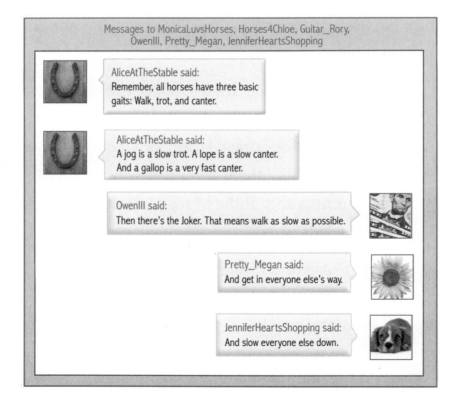

Messages to MonicaLuvsHorses, Horses4Chloe, Guitar_Rory, OwenIII, Pretty_Megan, JenniferHeartsShopping

AliceAtTheStable said:
Remember, all horses have three basic gaits: Walk, trot, and canter.

AliceAtTheStable said:
A jog is a slow trot. A lope is a slow canter. And a gallop is a very fast canter.

OwenIII said:
Then there's the Joker. That means walk as slow as possible.

Pretty_Megan said:
And get in everyone else's way.

JenniferHeartsShopping said:
And slow everyone else down.

When the trail got wider, Chloe and I stopped. We let the other horses pass us.

"I guess we're stuck bringing up the rear," I told Chloe.

"I don't mind," Chloe said. She made Rick-Rack slow down so we could ride side by side. It was easier to slow Rick-Rack down than to speed Joker up.

We both fell behind, trotted to catch up, and fell behind again.

"I'm glad this isn't a scary movie," I said. "The last guy in line always gets hurt."

Chloe laughed. "And nobody notices."

"I'd notice," a voice said. I turned around to see who was talking. It was a guy I'd never met. He was cute, with curly black hair and brown eyes. He was wearing a cool graphic t-shirt and comfortable-looking jeans.

"Who are you?" I asked.

"And where did you come from?" Chloe added.

"Ethan Westfield, from Holly Hills," the boy said.

"I meant where did you come from now," Chloe said. "I thought we were last in line."

"I doubled back to check on you," Ethan said. "Riding on trails can be dangerous."

I almost laughed. Chloe and I rode on the trails around Rock Creek all the time.

"We're fine," Chloe said. "You can go back to your friends."

"That's okay,"

Ethan said. "I'll stay with you and the slowpoke."

I frowned. For a second, I had thought this Ethan guy was being nice. But now I could see he was just like all the other horse snobs.

Chloe and I both tried to ignore Ethan. That was impossible.

"I've been getting Major ready for the Regional Horse Show," Ethan said, riding alongside us. He patted his dark brown horse. "Are you going, Chloe?"

"Probably," Chloe said.

"I'd love to ride in the Regional show," I said.

Ethan laughed. "You're kidding, right?" He shook his head.

Chloe frowned. "Are you making fun of Monica?" she asked.

Ethan looked hurt, as though Chloe was being mean. "She rides western," he said. "The Regional is English only."

"I ride English," I said. "This isn't my horse. I borrowed him."

"Her horse lost a shoe," Chloe explained. "She had to borrow Joker or miss the trail ride."

"Oh." Ethan shrugged. "Have you been showing long, Monica?"

"No," I said. I had ridden in small, local horse shows. I was pretty sure Ethan wouldn't be impressed.

It was soon pretty clear that Ethan Westfield was a horse snob. He kept bragging about all the prizes his horse had won.

"My dad built a special display case for my ribbons and trophies," Ethan said. "It takes up a whole wall."

Chloe glanced at me and rolled her eyes.

I thought maybe he'd get bored and leave. But once Ethan started talking, he didn't stop.

Ethan told us he thought Holly Hills Farm was better than Rock Creek Stables. He thought Chase was a better trainer than Mark, and he thought Chloe should switch barns.

"You'll start winning more ribbons if you switch to Holly Hills," Ethan said.

"I like Mark, and I like my friends at Rock Creek," Chloe said. "That's more important than ribbons."

Ethan didn't talk to me at all. He only wanted to talk to Chloe. Not that I wanted him to talk to me. He was one of the most stuck-up, self-centered, obnoxious boys I had ever met.

The worst part was that we couldn't get rid of him, no matter what we did. Chloe dropped a bunch of hints.

* * *

Chloe: "Monica and I have to talk about a school project."

Ethan: "What's the project? I know a lot about a lot of stuff. Maybe I can help."

* * *

Chloe: "Savannah is waving at you. I think she wants you to ride with her."

Ethan: "Savannah can't have everything she wants."

* * *

Chloe: "Three's a crowd, Ethan."

Ethan: "I know. Maybe Monica will leave."

* * *

Finally, we gave up.

The trail narrowed again, and Ethan had to drop back. Major didn't like leafy branches in his face.

Leaves didn't bother Joker, so I moved up to ride next to Chloe.

"Ethan is driving me crazy!" Chloe hissed. "He's like a mosquito buzzing around my ear. I wish he'd go bug Jennifer."

"He has a crush on you," I said.

Chloe shook her head. "Gross. I'm not interested."

"Even if you're not interested, he is," I told Chloe. "It's pretty obvious."

"We have to ditch Ethan," Chloe said, "but I don't want to hurt his feelings."

"Let's catch up to everyone else," I said.

"That won't help," Chloe said. "Joker has to jog to stay caught up."

I pretended to think about it. "Let's see," I said. "Should I jog Joker or listen to Ethan brag? Hmm. I think I'll jog."

Jogging Joker wasn't hard. The little horse wasn't as bouncy as the bigger horses. But staying with the group didn't solve our problem.

Ethan stayed right behind us. He would not go away and leave Chloe alone.

Messages to MonicaLuvsHorses

Horses4Chloe said:
HE IS DRIVING ME NUTS!!!!!!!!!!!!!!!

MonicaLuvsHorses said:
:(

Chapter Five

Chloe's
New Boyfriend

We left the woods, rode down a dirt road, and turned into a field.

"Who wants lunch?" Mark asked, turning his horse around to face the group.

We were all starving. Chloe and I shot our arms into the air.

"The Chuck Wagon is parked on that farm," Mr. Bristow told us. He pointed to a big red barn.

"Let's go," Owen said. "I'm starving."

"I hope we're not having bologna sandwiches," Jennifer mumbled. She shuddered. "Bologna makes me gag."

"Then don't eat it," Megan said. "Duh."

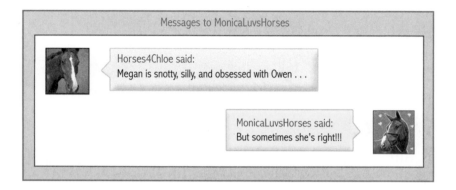

Messages to MonicaLuvsHorses

Horses4Chloe said:
Megan is snotty, silly, and obsessed with Owen . . .

MonicaLuvsHorses said:
But sometimes she's right!!!

We rode on the tractor track on the edge of the field. Chase Hogan, the Holly Hills riders, and some of the Rock Creek kids cantered ahead. I was in the back of the group, which was good since Joker didn't feel like going fast.

"They must be really hungry," I said.

"We don't mind if you go ahead with your friends, Ethan," Chloe said. "You'll get to the food faster. You're probably really hungry."

"I can wait," Ethan said.

Everyone slowed down to walk by the farm house. A dog ran out and barked at the horses.

Alice had told us that forests and farm country were full of loud noises, sudden movements, and strange objects. A good trail horse wouldn't get nervous and jumpy.

Major reared and bucked. Ethan's feet slipped out of his stirrups.

Blue Magic jumped sideways. Savannah almost fell off.

Rick-Rack snorted and pranced. He calmed down when Chloe patted his neck. "Easy, boy," she said. "It's just a silly dog."

Joker didn't even flinch. He just kept plodding along until we reached the barn. The Senior Center Cowboys were waiting there to serve lunch.

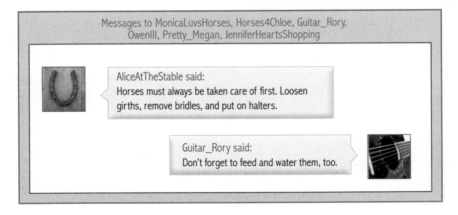

Messages to MonicaLuvsHorses, Horses4Chloe, Guitar_Rory, OwenIII, Pretty_Megan, JenniferHeartsShopping

AliceAtTheStable said:
Horses must always be taken care of first. Loosen girths, remove bridles, and put on halters.

Guitar_Rory said:
Don't forget to feed and water them, too.

Grandpa and Wally handed out sodas and box lunches. They had a special box for Jennifer.

"No bologna for you," Grandpa said, smiling. "Your sandwich is cheese only."

"With mustard or mayo?" Jennifer wrinkled her nose. "I don't like mustard. Did you cut the crusts off?"

"Next!" Grandpa yelled.

Chloe and I sat under a shady tree to eat. Ethan didn't ask if he could join us. He just sat down and started talking.

To Chloe.
Not to me. Not that I cared.

"Do you go to Rock Creek football games?" Ethan asked.

"No. I'm not a big football fan. But I like baseball," Chloe said.

I smiled. Ethan didn't know what I knew: Cameron Fuller, Chloe's maybe-secret-crush, played baseball for the Rock Creek Middle School team.

"I bet you'd like football if you knew more about it," Ethan said.

Chloe frowned at him. "I know what I like," she said.

"Do you like the band Bad Dog?" Ethan asked. "I went to their show last year. It was awesome."

"That's nice," Chloe said.

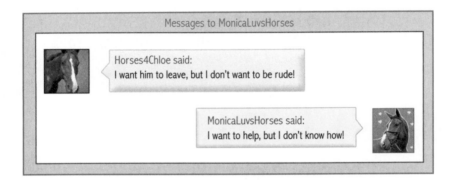

Messages to MonicaLuvsHorses

Horses4Chloe said:
I want him to leave, but I don't want to be rude!

MonicaLuvsHorses said:
I want to help, but I don't know how!

Messages to MonicaLuvsHorses

Guitar_Rory said:
Can I come over and sit with you and Chloe?

MonicaLuvsHorses said:
YES!!!!!!!

Rory walked over and sat down. Ethan ignored him, too.

"What's your favorite movie, Chloe?" Ethan asked. "I can't wait to see *Dragon Fliers*. Do you want to go with me?"

"Well, I — uh —" Chloe stuttered.

Rory narrowed his eyes. "Chloe's going to see that movie with me," he told Ethan.

"Is she your girlfriend?" Ethan asked.

Chloe hesitated. She never lies. Neither do I, unless it's an extreme emergency.

But Ethan was an extreme emergency. A fake Chloe-Rory romance was the only way to make him go away. I knew I had to jump in.

"Obviously she's his girlfriend," I said.

Ethan frowned at Chloe. "Why didn't you tell me you had a boyfriend?" he asked.

"You never asked," I told Ethan.

That was true. He'd been too busy being annoying and talking about himself.

Rory came to the rescue again. "Nobody knows about Chloe and me because I work at Rock Creek," he explained.

"Whatever," Ethan said. "You still could have told me before I wasted my entire day hanging out with you," he told Chloe. Then he picked up his sandwich and left. He sat down with Savannah and the other Holly Hills kids.

"Thanks, Rory," Chloe said, sighing with relief. "You totally saved the day."

"You're welcome," Rory said. "Ethan was being a pest."

"With a capital P and five exclamation points," I said.

"Just let me know if he bothers you again," Rory said. He winked. "I don't mind being your fake boyfriend," he added. "But right now I have to go help Alice."

"Well, that was very interesting," I said as Rory walked away.

"What do you mean?" Chloe asked.

"Rory doesn't have a crush on me," I explained.

Chloe laughed. "Of course he does," she said.

"No, Chloe, he doesn't," I told her. "He likes you!"

Chapter Six

Everybody
Hates Rory

Chloe and I had a lot more fun in the afternoon.
Rick-Rack and Joker became buddies, so we didn't
have to make them speed up or slow down. They
stayed together all by themselves.

We talked about riding in the Olympics or winning
the Kentucky Derby someday. We talked about our
other friends, and our families.

And the best part was, Ethan didn't come back.

Everyone was glad when we reached the campsite
in the Wilderness Preserve.

"Where's the food?" Owen asked. He rubbed his
stomach. "I'm starving."

"Over there," Rory said. He pointed.

The Senior Center Cowboys had set up tables and chairs in a big blue-and-white tent. One table was piled high with snacks. There were coolers full of ice and drinks.

"I ate a pound of trail dust." Megan coughed to clear her throat. "I need a soda."

"I'm wearing a pound of dust," Savannah said. She brushed dirt off her arms and jeans. "Where's the shower?"

"Over there," Alice told her, pointing to the pond.

"**Gross**," Savannah said. "Ponds are full of creepy creatures and slime!"

"Can we go swimming now?" asked a girl I didn't know.

"You bet. Right after we take care of the horses," Alice said. "You guys all know that the horses need to come first."

Jennifer got off her horse and made a sad face. "I ache all over. Will you take Hero, Rory?" she begged. "Please?"

Rory got off Jupiter and took Hero's reins. "You should walk around to loosen up your muscles," he told Jennifer.

"Okay," Jennifer said. I watched her limp toward the food tent.

Chloe and I walked Rick-Rack and Joker to a shady spot. We clipped their halters to the rope line and took off their saddles.

"Do you want to snack or swim first?" I asked Chloe.

"Snack," Chloe said. "Riding makes me super hungry."

The supply truck was parked by a cement tub. A water pump stood at one end of the tub. I pumped the handle and filled two buckets with water.

Chloe got the hay. We brushed our horses while they ate.

ClaudiaCristina said:
Hey, buddy!

MonicaLuvsHorses said:
Hey!

ClaudiaCristina said:
How's the trail ride going?

MonicaLuvsHorses said:
So far it's been pretty good. Riding is fun. But there's a really annoying guy here who keeps bugging me and Chloe. And we have to use an outhouse. Yuck!

ClaudiaCristina said:
What's an outhouse?

MonicaLuvsHorses said:
Um, you know . . . a toilet outside. Like an old-time porta-potty. Like people use at camp. What they used to use before people had bathrooms inside.

ClaudiaCristina said:
Ohhhhh. Ew.

ClaudiaCristna said:
Well, I have to go. Time to babysit. I just wanted to say hi.

MonicaLuvsHorses said:
I'll call you as soon as I get home!

ClaudiaCristina said:
Have FUN!!! :)

When Rory walked by, he was still leading two horses.

"Where's Jennifer?" I asked.

"I think she's in the outhouse," Rory said.

"Why would Jennifer go in the outhouse?" I wondered out loud. "It's probably full of spiders and bugs. And you know how she feels about spiders and bugs!"

"I guess she had to use it," Chloe said. "You know, when you gotta go . . ."

"Or maybe she's just hiding so Rory will take care of her horse," I said.

Rory tied Jupiter and Hero to the rope line. He took off both saddles and both bridles.

"Hey, Rory!" Owen yelled. "Bring me a bucket of water."

"And a soda for me!" Megan shouted.

"I need a hoof pick!" a Holly Hills rider yelled.

Rory gave Jupiter and Hero water first. Then he delivered the water and hoof pick.

Savannah's horse was tied beside Ethan's horse. Ethan and Savannah were sitting on a tree stump, talking to her. As Rory walked by, Savannah asked Rory to bring her some hay.

Rory brought hay to his horse, Jennifer's horse, and Savannah's horse. Another Holly Hills girl asked him for help grooming.

"Why is everyone picking on Rory?" I asked.

"Habit," Chloe said. "Owen orders Rory around all the time."

I frowned. "But Rory's not supposed to be working this weekend," I said.

"Maybe Mark and Alice didn't tell anyone that," Chloe said.

Mark was talking to the Senior Center Cowboys. Alice was helping the lesson kids. They didn't notice that Rory was doing way too many horse chores.

"We should say something," I said.

"I can't," Chloe said. "Ethan might tell his friends I'm sticking up for Rory because he's my boyfriend."

"So?" I said.

"Then it would get back to Owen and Megan," Chloe explained, "and I don't want that rumor going around school."

"Why not?" I asked. "You said yourself, Rory is really cute."

"It isn't true!" Chloe said. She blushed.

"And," she added, "I don't want it to get around."

I smiled. I knew what she meant. She didn't want Cameron to find out.

Chapter Seven

The Boss
of the Chuck Wagon

Messages to MonicaLuvsHorses

GrandpaJones1945 said:
You and Chloe better hurry up! We're running out of food over here.

MonicaLuvsHorses said:
We'll be right there. Save me some potato salad!

Grandpa was on duty in the mess tent. He grinned when Chloe and I walked in. "Are you having a good time?" he asked.

"Fantastic!" I said.

I gave him two thumbs up. "Joker is a great trail horse, just like you said."

"Are you sorry you called him lazy and scruffy?" Grandpa teased.

"He is lazy and scruffy," I teased back. "But he's easy to take care of, and he does what I want him to."

Thinking about taking care of Joker made me think of how Rory was being forced to help everyone else. I sighed.

Grandpa frowned. "What's wrong?" he asked.

Chloe and I looked at each other.

"Mark gave Rory the weekend off so he could enjoy the campout," I said.

"But some of the kids are bossing him around like they do at the barn," Chloe explained.

"That's not fair," Grandpa said. He squinted and rubbed his chin. "So I'd better do something about it."

"What are you going to do?" I asked.

"You'll see," Grandpa said with a twinkle in his eye.

While Grandpa walked over to Mark, Chloe and I sat down at an old picnic table outside the tent. We could see the whole campsite.

First Grandpa spoke to Mark. Then he marched over to the rope line. He pulled Rory aside and whispered in his ear.

Rory nodded and ran over to join us.

"What's going on?" Chloe asked as he sat down.

"Monica's grandpa told me to take a break," Rory said. "Mark's orders."

Grandpa stayed by the rope line. He spoke in a gruff voice. "Listen up!" he called out. Everyone turned to look.

"This trail ride has rules," Grandpa continued. "Rule number one: Everyone takes care of his or her own horse."

"You're not the boss of us," Owen said, folding his arms in front of his chest.

"No, but I'm the boss of the Chuck Wagon," Grandpa said. "Nobody eats until their horse chores are done."

"But you have to feed us!" Megan whined.

"I will," Grandpa told her. "As soon as you feed and water your horse."

Nobody moved for a minute. Then everyone got busy.

Owen and Megan rushed to the hay bales. Jennifer tried to duck behind a truck, but Chase handed her a bucket.

I noticed that Savannah and Ethan were standing next to their horses, but it seemed like they were arguing. Savannah threw up her hands and stomped away.

Ethan untied his horse. Then he walked over and tied the horse back up next to Joker and Rick-Rack. Then he stood there, staring at his horse.

Rory nudged Chloe. "Do you want Ethan to move his horse?" he asked.

Chloe shook her head. "That's okay," she said. She looked at Ethan and frowned. "It looks like he needs help," she added. "I guess I should go see what his problem is."

"I'll go with you," I said.

Ethan smiled when he saw us. "I took Major's saddle and bridle off, but the grooms at Holly Hills do everything else. What should I do next?" he asked.

"Water, then hay, and then brush him," I said.

"And don't forget to clean out his feet," Chloe added.

Chloe and I helped carry everything from the supply truck, but we let Ethan do the work.

Major liked to slosh his nose in his water bucket. Ethan's shirt got wet.

Major pawed his hay. Ethan had to shake the packed grass to loosen it. A hundred bits stuck to his jeans.

The dust on Major's coat made Ethan sneeze.

"No wonder Savannah wanted me to groom Blue Magic," Ethan said. "This is hard work."

"Major worked hard for you all day," I pointed out.

"You're right," Ethan said with a sheepish grin.

Soon, everyone was done grooming the horses. We each stood next to our horse while Mark and Chase inspected our work.

Owen had to clean Merlin's feet again.

Megan had to refill Dandy's water bucket.

Savannah had to keep brushing until Blue Magic's saddle mark was gone.

Rick-Rack, Joker, and Major were perfect.

"Cool!" Ethan said.

He had done everything right, and I could tell he was proud.

I watched Ethan high-five Rory.

Messages to Horses4Chloe

MonicaLuvsHorses said:
Maybe he's not so bad after all!

Chapter Eight

Stuck
Like Glue

Everyone scattered when the inspection ended.

Alice and some of the kids went swimming. Rory volunteered to be the lifeguard.

Owen, Megan, Savannah, and most of the other owners ran for the mess tent. They wanted to scarf snacks, guzzle sodas, and relax.

The Senior Center Cowboys had already stacked large logs for the bonfire. Grandpa looked at the pile of wood. "We need kindling," he said. "Who will go gather some more wood?"

Chloe and I raised our hands. "We will, Grandpa," I said.

Ethan walked over from the mess tent. "I'll help too," he said.

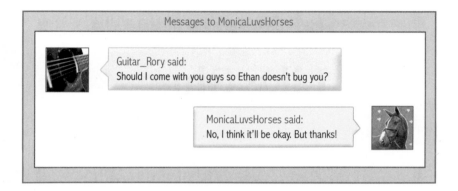

The three of us walked into the woods and started grabbing twigs and small branches. "Let's make a big pile," Chloe suggested. She dropped an armful of sticks.

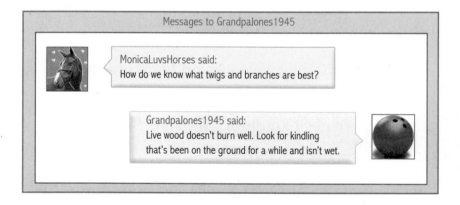

Ethan snapped a broken branch off a tree. He started to put it onto the pile.

"Not that one," I said.

Ethan frowned. "What's wrong with it?" he asked.

"It came off a live tree," I explained. "It won't burn as well."

"What else should I know?" Ethan asked.

"Watch out for thorns," Chloe said.

"And rotted wood with ants," I added. "Ants are tiny, but they bite big."

Chloe and I went in opposite directions. I guess Ethan didn't want to be alone in the woods, because he followed me.

"Have you always liked horses?" Ethan asked.

"Yep," I said.

"Do your Pine Tree friends ride?" Ethan asked.

"Nope," I said. "I'm the only one who likes horses."

"Oh. Does anyone in your family ride?" he asked.

"No," I said. Ethan was starting to annoy me.

I turned to move away, and my foot snagged on a blackberry vine. I tripped.

"Be careful!"
Ethan said.

He grabbed my arm and stopped my fall. "Are you okay?"

I nodded. "Yes, thank you," I told him.

Now I couldn't ditch Ethan. He had saved me from a hundred bramble scratches.

"Let's go find Chloe," I said. I picked up a few more branches and started walking back.

Chloe was waiting by the pile. "I think we have enough wood," she said. "Let's carry it back and go for a swim."

We delivered the wood in two trips. Then we got our backpacks from the truck.

In one of the sleeping tents, Chloe and I changed into our bathing suits.

Ethan was waiting when we came out. He had changed into his suit too. Chloe and I looked at each other and rolled our eyes.

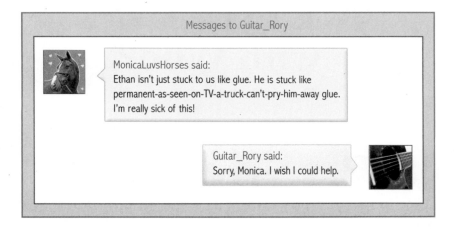

Messages to Guitar_Rory

MonicaLuvsHorses said:
Ethan isn't just stuck to us like glue. He is stuck like permanent-as-seen-on-TV-a-truck-can't-pry-him-away glue. I'm really sick of this!

Guitar_Rory said:
Sorry, Monica. I wish I could help.

As we headed toward the pond, a shriek stopped us in our tracks. Jennifer was freaking out near the mess tent.

"Wasp!" Jennifer cried out. "Get it away! Get it away!" She waved her arms and spun in circles.

The horses freaked out. They pulled on the rope line, and it broke.

Suddenly, all the horses were loose.

Chapter Nine

You're
with Who?

"Come back!"

Megan screamed. "Dandy, come back!"

She ran after her horse, but he was too fast to catch.

"Stop them!" Savannah yelled.

The horses raced around the large field, kicking up their heels. It had been a hard day for them, too. They wanted to play.

Rick-Rack ran and bucked with the herd.

Joker just raised his head and snorted. He didn't seem like he wanted to run.

"They won't go far," Alice called. "The Wilderness Preserve is fenced in. They'll be okay."

The horses circled back. Rory tried to grab Hero, but Jennifer's horse jumped clear and ran on.

"Where's Major?" Ethan asked, looking all around.

"He's over there," I told him. I pointed. Major was grazing by the pond. Alice and some of the lesson kids tried to sneak up on him, but the horse started running before they could catch him.

Merlin was rolling in the dirt to scratch his back.

"I just finished brushing him," Owen complained. "Somebody do something!"

"Like what?" Megan asked. "The horses won't come to anyone!"

Mark looked at me. "No, they won't. Monica, who will horses come to?" he asked me.

I frowned, thinking. Then I realized what he meant. "Another horse!" I yelled. "They'll come to another horse." I didn't waste a second. I ran for the broken rope line.

Joker hadn't gone far. He let me catch him, and he stood still while I put on his bridle. Then he stayed still while I scrambled onto his bare back.

"Okay, Joker," I said. "Let's show these people what a good cow pony can do."

Joker and I started trotting around the field. I didn't have to chase Rick-Rack. He walked right up to Joker.

"Thanks, Monica!" Chloe exclaimed. "I'll bridle Rick-Rack so I can help."

"Catch Major next," Ethan said. "I'll help too."

Major wasn't as easy as Rick-Rack. He would let Joker get close. Then he would just trot away. Joker and I kept trying until Major finally stopped long enough for Ethan to walk over.

With Chloe and Ethan helping, it only took ten minutes to round up the rest of the horses.

"Good job, Monica," Alice said. "That was some really quick thinking and hard work."

"Joker did most of the work," I said. I bent down and hugged Joker's neck. He twitched an ear.

"I guess that old cow pony is good for something, huh?" Grandpa said. He winked at me.

"I guess so," I said, giving Joker a kiss on top of his head.

"That was fun!" Chloe said. Her face was red with excitement.

"What should we do next?" Ethan asked.

"Can we take the horses in the pond, Alice?" I asked.

"You can try," Alice said. "They might not want to go."

Several other kids got their horses ready and followed us, but I noticed that none of the Holly Hills kids did. Except Ethan. But no one seemed to care. The horses were thirsty after their wild run, and they all stopped to take a drink.

"Is the water very deep?" Chloe asked.

"Only in the middle," another kid said.

Ethan's horse waded in up to his ankles and stopped.

Rick-Rack got wet to his knees before he refused to go deeper.

"I bet Joker likes to swim," Chloe said.

"Let's see," I said.

Joker went into the water past his knees and then past his belly. When he couldn't touch bottom, he started horse paddling!

"He's swimming!" I yelled. I held onto Joker's mane so I wouldn't slide off. Then Joker swam back to shallow water and whickered to Rick-Rack.

"He wants to play!" I told Chloe.

"Come on, boy," Chloe said. Rick-Rack pranced for a minute. Then he plunged in.

Both horses pawed the water, splashing Chloe and me. Most of the other horses finally walked into the pond. Some only went in up to their knees. Jupiter and Major swam in the deep part.

"That is so cool!" Ethan said, laughing.

We played in the water until Grandpa announced that dinner was almost ready.

Ethan and I were the first ones back from the pond. The trainers had fixed the rope line.

Savannah was waiting next to it.

"What's up?" Ethan asked.

Savannah crossed her arms and pressed her lips together. She narrowed her eyes and tapped her foot. "How come you'd rather pal around with the barn help and lesson kids than hang out with your friends?" she asked him.

Ethan hesitated. Then he put his arm around my shoulders!

"I'm with Monica this weekend," he told her.

My mouth dropped open. I couldn't speak.

Savannah looked me up and down. "Oh," she said. Then she turned and flounced off.

Ethan exhaled with relief.

I was furious!

First Ethan had chased Chloe. After she shot him down he had chased me.

Was he trying to make Savannah jealous? Or did he just want something to brag about at school?

"Park your horse somewhere else, Ethan," I said. "I'm not your weekend girlfriend."

MVH

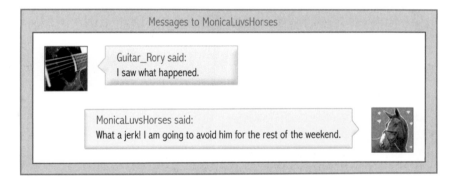

Messages to MonicaLuvsHorses

Guitar_Rory said:
I saw what happened.

MonicaLuvsHorses said:
What a jerk! I am going to avoid him for the rest of the weekend.

"I thought you and Ethan were getting along," Chloe said as we sat down to eat dinner. "How come he's sitting with the Holly Hills kids?"

I shook my head. "I don't want to talk about it," I said. I hoped Chloe would just assume I was sick of Ethan. I didn't want to tell her what had happened.

Luckily, Rory changed the subject. "Your mom's potato salad is really good," he told me.

"Yeah, it goes great with the corn on the cob!" Alice added.

Chloe bit into her hamburger. "I'm really hungry after this long day," she said. "Who knew doing so much riding would be so tiring!"

After dinner, Mark made an announcement. "The Senior Center Cowboys will clean up," he said. "Grab your jackets and flashlights. The campfire starts in fifteen minutes!"

After we got our jackets, Chloe had to use the outhouse. I waited outside.

That's when Ethan ambushed me.

"Can I talk to you?" Ethan pleaded. "Please?"

"You've got one minute," I said sternly. Ethan had been annoying me all day. I wasn't going to let him spoil the bonfire, too.

"I'm sorry I told Savannah we were together," Ethan said.

"Why did you tell her that?" I asked.

"Because I didn't want to tell her the real reason I like to hang out with you and Chloe," Ethan said. "In case it hurt her feelings."

"What is the real reason?" I asked.

"You guys have more fun," Ethan said, shrugging. "My horse friends take themselves way too seriously, especially Savannah."

"Some of the Rock Creek riders do, too," I said.

"I know," Ethan agreed. "Owen and Megan are too worried about winning the Most Valuable Horse trophy to have a good time. Who needs that?"

"Not me," I said.

"Me neither," Ethan said.

"Do you want me to pretend I'm your girlfriend?" I asked.

Ethan smiled and shook his head. "No, it's stupid to care what Savannah thinks," he admitted.

I nodded. Just like I was stupid to care what other kids thought about Joker. And then I realized something else. Chloe and Rory and I had misjudged Ethan the same way.

Chloe, Ethan, and I walked to the campfire circle together. Rory sat down between me and Chloe.

Chloe looked at me with a smug smile. I knew what she was thinking.

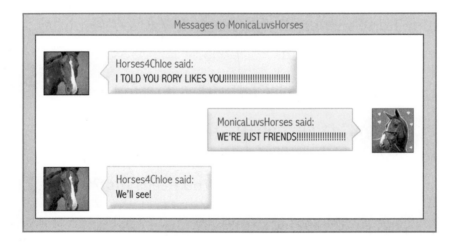

The Senior Center Cowboys handed out graham crackers, chocolate bars, marshmallows, and toasting sticks. Then they sang dorky old camp songs. Everyone ate s'mores and sang along.

Savannah, Owen, and Megan looked bored until Mark stood up. He held the Most Valuable Horse trophy for everyone to see.

"There are many different types of horses," Mark said, "and they are all good at different jobs. A good trail horse stays calm no matter what happens."

"And a good trail horse is safe and easy to ride," Chase added. "Only one horse lived up to that today."

"We're proud to present the Most Valuable Horse award to —" Mark paused to build up the suspense. Then he said, "Monica Murray and Joker!"

"Joker won?" I squealed and jumped up and down. "I have to call Buck!" I told Chloe and Rory.

I got Buck's phone number from Grandpa. When I called, I told Buck what had happened and how Joker had helped us round up all the horses.

On the other end of the line, Buck laughed. "That's great news, Monica," he said. "Joker is a fine horse."

"He is," I agreed. Then I asked, "So do you have a nice place to keep the trophy?"

Buck was silent for a second. "Well," he said slowly, "there's a certain thirteen-year-old girl who deserves that trophy just as much as my old plug does. I think you should keep it, Monica."

"Really?" I said. A huge smile stretched across my face. "Thanks, Buck!"

I handed the trophy to Chloe. "Can you hold this for me?" I asked.

"Where are you going?" Chloe asked.

"To give Joker a big hug," I said. "And carrots. Lots and lots of carrots."

Messages to Horses4Chloe

MonicaLuvsHorses said:
I had an amazing weekend!

Horses4Chloe said:
Me too! :) See you soon!

Monica's SECRET Blog

Sunday, 9:30 p.m.

This weekend was a blast. Me, my friends from the stable, our horses, and two whole days of riding and having fun.

I met a bunch of new people, riders from Holly Hills. One of them, Ethan, turned out to be a really cool guy. At first I thought Chloe and I were going to have to get Grandpa to make him leave us alone or something, but after a while he relaxed. That's when I realized he wasn't a total jerk.

Not that I like Ethan. I mean, I do like him. I don't like-like him. Seriously.

I think I might like someone else THAT WAY.

I don't want to say who. I'll just say it's a guy, and he's a friend of mine.

Anyway, the second day of the trail ride was just as fun as the first, except that I was super tired.

We stayed up too late telling ghost stories and eating s'mores.

Rory made me a triple-decker s'more. That's right. A graham cracker, topped with chocolate and marshmallow, with a graham cracker on top. Times three. All smushed together. It was amazing!

But I kind of felt sick afterward.

I better get going. I still have to finish my homework for tomorrow. I definitely would not want to go on a trail ride every weekend. I'd never get any homework done!

love,

Monica

 1 comment from Chloe: I think I know who you like!!!!!! :) :) And I think he likes you too!!!

Leave a comment:

| | Name (required) |

MONICA MURRAY

 AVATAR

SCREEN NAME: MonicaLuvsHorses

ABOUT ME:

Activities:	HORSEBACK RIDING!, hanging out with my friends, watching TV, listening to music, writing, shopping, sleeping in on weekends, swimming, watching movies . . . all the usual stuff
Favorite music:	Tornado, Bad Dog, Haley Hover
Favorite books:	A Tree Grows in Brooklyn, Harry Potter, Diary of Anne Frank, Phantom High
Favorite movies:	Heartbreak High, Alien Hunter, Canyon Stallion
Favorite TV shows:	Musical Idol, MyWorld, Boutique TV, Island
Fan of:	Pine Tree Cougars, Rock Creek Stables, Pizza Palace, Red Brick Inn, K Brand Jeans, Miss Magazine, The Pinecone Press, Horse Newsletter Quarterly, Teen Scene, Boutique Magazine, Haley Hover
Groups:	Peter for President!!!, Bring Back T-Shirt Tuesday, I Listen to WHCR In The Morning, Laughing Makes Everything Better!, I Have A Stepsister, Ms. Stark's Homeroom, Princess Patsy Is Annoying!, Haley Should Have Won on Musical Idol!, Pine Tree Eighth Grade, Mr. Monroe is the Best Science Teacher of All Time
Quotes:	No hour of life is wasted that is spent in the saddle. ~Winston Churchill
	A horse is worth more than riches. ~Spanish proverb

View Photos of Me (100)

Edit My Profile

My Friends (236)

INFORMATION:

Relationship Status:
Single

Astrological Sign:
Taurus

Current City:
Pine Tree

Family Members:
Traci Gregory
Logan Gregory
Frank Jones
Angela Gregory

Best Friends:
Claudia Cortez
Becca McDougal
Chloe Granger
Adam Locke
Rory Weber
Tommy Patterson
Peter Wiggins

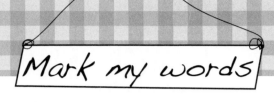

bridle (BRYE-duhl)—straps that fit around a horse's head and are used to control it

canter (KAN-tur)—to run at a speed between a gallop and a trot

equipment (i-KWIP-muhnt)—tools

halter (HAWL-tur)—a strap used to lead a horse

inspection (in-SPEK-shuhn)—a check or exam

mount (MOUNT)—to get on a horse

pasture (PASS-chur)—grazing land for animals

preserve (pri-ZURV)—a piece of land that is protected

reins (RAYNZ)—straps attached to a bridle that control a horse

stirrup (STUR-uhp)—a loop that hangs down from a saddle to hold a rider's foot

tack (TAK)—equipment needed to ride a horse

trophy (TROH-fee)—a prize (often a small statue or a metal cup) given to a winner

valuable (VAL-yoo-uh-buhl)—very important

TEXT 911!

With your friends, help solve these problems.

1

Messages to Text 911!

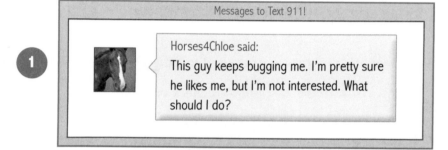

Horses4Chloe said:

This guy keeps bugging me. I'm pretty sure he likes me, but I'm not interested. What should I do?

2

Messages to Text 911!

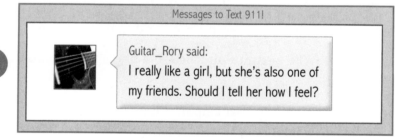

Guitar_Rory said:

I really like a girl, but she's also one of my friends. Should I tell her how I feel?

3

Messages to Text 911!

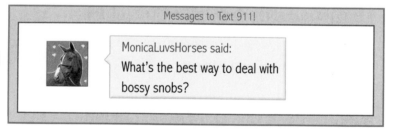

MonicaLuvsHorses said:

What's the best way to deal with bossy snobs?

You can write too.

Some people write in journals or diaries. I have a secret blog. Here are some writing prompts to help you write your own blog or diary entries.

1 I rode in my first trail ride. Write about something you just did for the first time. What was it? How did you feel afterward?

2 I love spending time with my grandpa. Write about one of your grandparents.

3 Write about a time you spent a weekend or a night away from home. What did you do?

ABOUT THE AUTHOR: DIANA G. GALLAGHER

Just like Monica, Diana G. Gallagher has loved riding horses since she was a little girl. And like Becca, she is an artist. Like Claudia, she often babysits little kids — usually her grandchildren. Diana has wanted to be a writer since she was twelve, and she has written dozens of books, including the Claudia Cristina Cortez series. She lives in Florida with her husband, five dogs, three cats, and one cranky parrot.

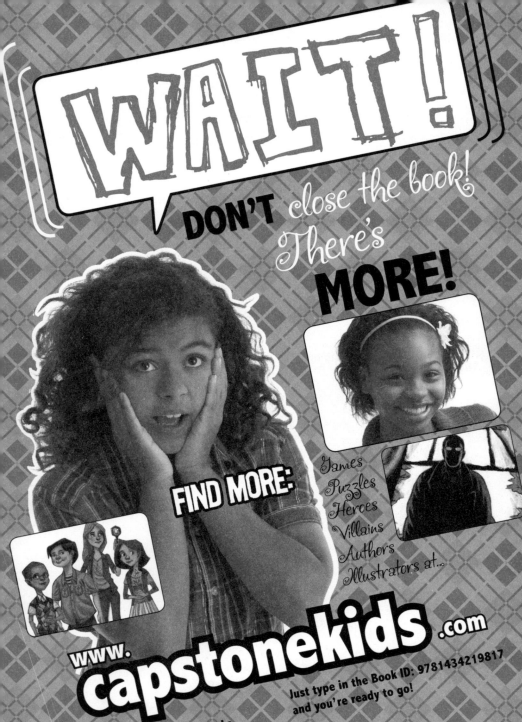